everywhere,
wonder

To our parents
Our Egypt, our blue balloons

IMPRINT
A part of Macmillan Children's Publishing Group, a division of Macmillan Publishing Group, LLC

ABOUT THIS BOOK
The art for this book is a digital collage of sampled watercolor washes done in Adobe Photoshop using a Cintiq 13 HD tablet. The text was set in ITC Cheltenham, and the display type is Olivier and Grumpy. The book was edited by Erin Stein and designed by Natalie C. Sousa. The production was supervised by Raymond Ernesto Colón, and the production editor was Melinda Ackell.

Library of Congress Cataloging-in-Publication Data
Names: Swanson, Matthew, 1974- author. | Behr, Robbi, illustrator.
Title: Everywhere, wonder / by Matthew Swanson ; illustrated by Robbi Behr.
Description: First edition. | New York : Imprint, 2017. | Summary: "A book
   for all ages about noticing the wonder and beauty in the world both near
   and far"— Provided by publisher.
Identifiers: LCCN 2016006416 | ISBN 9781250087959 (hardcover)
Subjects: | CYAC: Curiosities and wonders—Fiction. | BISAC: JUVENILE FICTION
   / People & Places / General. | JUVENILE FICTION / Social Issues / New
   Experience.
Classification: LCC PZ7.S9719 Ev 2017 | DDC [E]—dc23
LC record available at https://lccn.loc.gov/2016006416

Our books may be purchased in bulk for promotional, educational, or business use.
Please contact your local bookseller or the Macmillan Corporate and
Premium Sales Department at (800) 221-7945 ext. 5442 or by
e-mail at MacmillanSpecialMarkets@macmillan.com.

Imprint logo designed by Amanda Spielman

First Edition—2017

10 9 8 7 6 5 4 3 2 1

mackids.com

Travel these pages and take a close look.
You are the reason I've written this book.
Take what you find here and live it today,
then wake up tomorrow and give it away.
But if this book is not your own,
read and return. Don't take it home.

everywhere, wonder

written by
MATTHEW SWANSON

illustrated by
ROBBI BEHR

【Imprint】
MAKE YOUR MARK

New York

I have a story to share.
It is a little gift from me to you.

You might not know it,
but you have a story, too.

You'll find it in the things you stop to notice.

The world is full of people and places and things, all of them interesting. All of them beautiful.

You never know what you might see—
or where your mind might take you.

So keep your eyes wide open as you go.

In Egypt, there are pyramids.

In Arizona, there are canyons.

In the jungles of Brazil are leaves
so plentiful and green
that light can barely reach
the ground below.

In the high hills of Japan are gardens full of wind-worn rocks and clean white sand, but not a single flower.

In Kenya, there are hot, dry savannas
filled with zebras and
blue wildebeest.

In Alaska, there are cold, wet waters
filled with seals and sockeye salmon.

In the middle of the Coral Sea,
there is a roaring storm that no one will ever hear.

On the near side of the moon,
there is a quiet footprint that no rains will ever wash away.

In Sheboygan, there is a tractor mechanic named Shirley who has thirty-seven friends.

On the North Pole, there is a cold and lonesome bear,
wishing for some company.

You want to go see him, of course, to let him know he's not alone,
but your bike won't get you there and back by bedtime.

Still, you noticed him, didn't you?
He walked off this page and into your head.

Now he is part of your story.

There are other wonders
yet to find, not so far from
where you are right now.

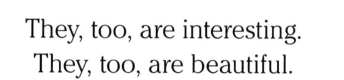

They, too, are interesting.
They, too, are beautiful.

Stop to really look, and you will see them.

In the highest part of the tree is an
unexpected gift—a blue balloon
that must have slipped
from someone's fingers.

In the deepest part of the pool is sunken treasure—
a shiny dime that must have tumbled from someone's pocket.

Will you save it or spend it
or leave it there for someone else to find?

In the grocery store are aisles and shelves and stacks of cans.
You have to look so carefully to find the one you want.

In your bowl of steaming soup is just one noodle
that doesn't match the others. Where do you think it came from?

On the playground is a sturdy line
of bright black ants, carrying
their supper home.

Under the bridge is a gently
rolling river, floating a blue
glass bottle out to sea.

Perhaps it holds a message.
What does it say?
Who could it be for?

In the busy town are sidewalks full of swiftly moving people
who somehow never seem to collide.

In the quiet countryside are miles of open, empty roads that somehow never seem to end.

Where do they go?
Someday you may find out.

In the hallway is a spotted dog
that turns golden as the sun sets
through the window.

In the bedroom is a doorknob
that makes rainbows
when the reading lamp clicks on.

Now the lamp is off and
the moon is up.

You close your eyes
and see them again—the things you noticed today.

All of these together are your story.

Dream with them
awhile.

When you wake up in the morning,
open your eyes and open your window
and let your story out into the world.

It is a little gift from you to me.

Now my story is complete.

But yours is just beginning.